To my children and grandchildren.
You are my superheroes.

MY SUPER POWERS: WORD OF KNOWLEDGE

Illustration design by Dan McCollam
Comic images © 2013 Pixton.com

Cover design by Paul Wayland Lee.
PaulWaylandLee.com

Published by Sounds of the Nations.
SoundsoftheNations.com

ISBN-13: 978-1494212513
ISBN-10: 149421251X

DEAR PARENT,

My Super Powers is a series of children's books based on the nine gifts of the Holy Spirit mentioned in 1 Corinthians 12:8-9. I believe that children can and should be activated in the gifts of the Spirit at an early age.

To help you facilitate that activation, each *My Super Powers* book contains the following features:

1. A **SUPER POWER STORY** sharing how Timmy and his mother discover one of the gifts of the Spirit and what that gift could look like in the life of a child.

2. A **BIBLE TIME PAGE** providing Bible references for further exploration of the featured gift of the Spirit and for any Bible stories mentioned within the book.

3. A **TALK TIME PAGE** for sparking discussions with your children about the story and their own spiritual gifts.

4. A **PRAYER TIME PAGE** to pray for gifts of the Holy Spirit and then activate them in a simple, practical way.

Word of Knowledge

by Dan McCollam

One day Timmy was
jumping in bed
with one of Mom's pots
on top of his head.
"Timmy, be careful!
You'll fall!" Mom said,
"And why is that pot
on top of your head?"

Timmy stretched out one arm,
and he spoke really strange,
"I'm a mind reader called
Dr. Deranged!
I see the thoughts that float
through your head.
I know your words
before they are said."

"Don't be so silly,"
Mom said with a nod.
"The only one who knows what
I'm thinking is God.
But there are times when God
shares His thoughts with you."

Timmy stopped jumping
and asked, "Is this true?"

So they sat on the bed
and they opened the Book.
They leafed through the pages
as they both took a look.

"It's called Word of Knowledge,"
said Mom to her son.
"It's a gift of the Spirit
from First Corinthians."

"The Word of Knowledge is when at times God will show secret information that one otherwise would not know..."

"...like things from your past,

...or the name of your street."

"... or the name of your mom,"

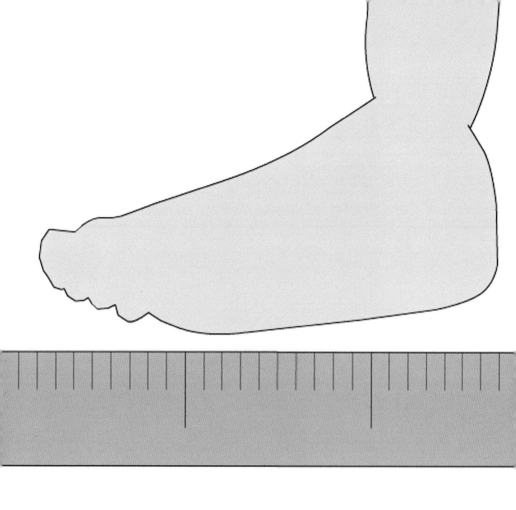

"...or the size of your feet."

Remember when Jesus met
Nathanael one day?
He saw a young man
whom he liked right away.
Jesus said, "I saw you
sitting under a tree
before you ever came here
to meet me."

"That's just where I was
before I came here,"
said Nathanael with shock
as it now became clear.
"We've looked for our Savior;
you must be the One!
Now I believe
that you are God's son!"

Jesus answered,
"Is this the reason
that you believe?
Because I saw you
under the tree?"

When we use this gift
to show what God knows,
then people believe,
and their faith grows.
People can see
that God still speaks today
to those who will listen with faith
as they pray.

Timmy tore the pot
right off of his head,
and he looked at the Book
that now sat on his bed.

He believed God to show things
that could not easily be known
when he asked for this gift
of God's for his own.

Now Timmy had power
to show God is real,
that He knows what people
are thinking,
what they've done,
how they feel...

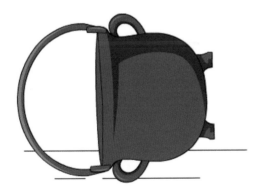

And his heart felt bigger
inside of his chest.
He felt warm and special
and really...
really...
blessed.

THE
END

BIBLE TIME

The spiritual gift of Word of Knowledge is found in **1 Corinthians 12:8**. The Word of Knowledge is the ability to know secret information by the power of God's Spirit.

Our *My Super Powers* story on Word of Knowledge includes an example from the life of Nathanael. Philip invited Nathanael to come and meet Jesus, but Nathanael didn't believe there was anything special about Jesus. Philip told him to come and see for himself.

As he approached, Jesus told Nathanael something about where he had been that Jesus could not have known except by the power of the Holy Spirit – this is a Word of Knowledge. The revealing of this supernatural knowledge led Nathanael to believe Jesus was indeed the Messiah.

Read more about it in John 1:45-51. Read 1 Corinthians 2:9-16 to learn more.

TALK TIME

What did Nathanael think about Jesus when Philip first invited him?

What did he think about Jesus after he met him?

What changed Nathanael's mind about Jesus?

One of the purposes of the spiritual gift of Word of Knowledge is to help people who don't believe in Jesus to understand that God really does know our thoughts and our lives. When we share information or secrets of the heart that no one could know but that person and God, then they have the opportunity to believe in Jesus.

How does the gift of Word of Knowledge change people's mind about Jesus?

PRAYER TIME

Ask God for the spiritual gift of Word of Knowledge and then wait for a moment.

While you were asking and waiting did any pictures or ideas come into your head?

Now let's try an activation experiment. Ask God to show you three things about your parent when he or she was younger. Maybe you will see a picture, or hear a name, or just have an idea pop into your head.

Share any pictures or ideas that you got with your parent. If any of the information you share with your parent was true and something that you did not know before, then you just experienced the spiritual gift of Word of Knowledge?

Thank God for anything He shared with you and be watching for Words of Knowledge.

OTHER SUPER POWERS STORIES

Word of Wisdom

Gift of Faith

Gifts of Healing

Working of Miracles

Gift of Prophecy

Discernment of Spirits

Gift of Tongues

Interpretation of Tongues

46256509R00022

Made in the USA
Charleston, SC
14 September 2015